Arjun and his village in India

Written and illustrated by

CAROL BARKER

Oxford   New York   Toronto   Melbourne

OXFORD UNIVERSITY PRESS · 1979

Oxford University Press, Walton Street, Oxford OX2 6DP

OXFORD   LONDON   GLASGOW

NEW YORK   TORONTO   MELBOURNE   WELLINGTON

KUALA LUMPUR   SINGAPORE   JAKARTA   HONG KONG   TOKYO

DELHI   BOMBAY   CALCUTTA   MADRAS   KARACHI

NAIROBI   DAR ES SALAAM   CAPE TOWN

This book is dedicated to
Aruna & Sanjit Roy, Manya Lindsay,
also to Dr Arti Sawhny, Pramod Sabharwal,
Giriraj Singh, and to all my other friends in India.

Thanks are due to OXFAM for sponsoring
my travel in India, and making this book possible.
Anyone buying this book will be helping and contributing
towards OXFAM's work, and aid to India.

International Year of the Child 1979

The United Kingdom Association for the International Year of
the Child 1979 welcomes the publication of this book
as a contribution to building awareness of the rights, needs
and hopes of children. The views expressed are those of
the author and not necessarily of the Association.

British Library Cataloguing in Publication Data

Barker, Carol
  Arjun and his village in India.
    1. Rajasthan, India – Social life and customs
    – Juvenile literature
    2. Country life – India – Rajasthan –
  Juvenile literature
  I. Title
954'.4   DS422.R26   79-40574

ISBN 0-19-279734-4

Printed in Great Britain by W. S. Cowell, Ltd, at The Butter Market, Ipswich

Arjun lives in Tilonia, a village in Rajasthan, which is a state of north west India. The land is usually dry and parched, as the monsoon rains do not last long there. On one side of Tilonia are bare rock-mountains where vultures and kites live, and miles and miles of arid wasteland. On the other side, where wells have been built, are green fertile fields, and trees and flowers. Here wild peacocks strut alongside their flocks of peahens, and green parrots fly.

   Arjun himself told me about his family and his own life in the village. 'My father's name is Ghisa-Baba Jat, and my mother is called Kani Jat. I'm twelve, and I've got two older sisters and two brothers and a baby sister younger than me.'

'My grandparents and four uncles and their wives and children live with us too. We have houses next to each other round a communal courtyard, and we share the same kitchen and take turns to do the cooking. Grandfather is head of the household but when he dies his eldest son, my father, will be head of the household. My father is a farmer and he's got twenty-five bighas of land, and my uncles have each got twenty-five bighas too.' (A bigha is about half an acre, so Arjun's family owns about 60 acres of land altogether.)

'We've got two wells on our land. It takes two pairs of bullocks working
together to draw water out of them to irrigate the land. We've also
got twenty-five cows and buffaloes, and fifty goats.

'Every day my mother and my four aunts get up at 3.30 a.m. Three
of them go to fetch water while the other one and my mother sweep out
the house. Then mother grinds maize or wheat flour between two
large round stones, turning the top stone with a wooden handle very
fast round and round. My aunt churns curd which has been left to set
overnight and makes butter out of it. Then mother lights the cooking
fire and makes rotis, fried chapattis—like pancakes—from the flour for
breakfast and to take for lunch. She also makes a maize porridge which
we call ghat.

'Father and my uncles get up a bit later, about 4.30 a.m. They wash
themselves and then two of my uncles go to milk the cows and see to
the goats, while the other two and father get their farming tools ready
and load them on the cart—the plough, if it's needed, scythes, hoes, the
big leather pouch for drawing water, and a leather sling to scare away
the birds.

'After that they have breakfast—chapattis with curd and a bowl of
ghat. The two uncles load the milk churns on to their bicycles and
ride to Tilonia railway station to catch the 6 a.m. train with the other
milkmen from the village to go to Kishangarh and Ajmer to sell the
milk.

'Mother wakes me and my brothers and sisters and cousins at 7 a.m.
I get washed and then milk two of the goats—we drink the milk in the

evening. Then mother gives us our breakfast—roti and curd, and ghat with jaggery, which is a sort of sugary fudge. Only after we children have eaten are mother and the other women allowed to have their breakfast. Then mother gives us $1\frac{1}{2}$ chapattis each and some chilli peppers in a cloth to eat for lunch.

'After he's had his breakfast, father harnesses two of the bullocks to the cart with the tools in it and adds to the load some hay or green fodder for the animals. Then two of them drive out to the fields while his other brother follows with the second pair of bullocks.

'Then it's our turn to collect the other animals. My elder sisters and cousins take the cows and buffaloes off one way and I and my young cousin Basanti get the goats out of their pen, and drive them through the village streets.'

It is now about 8 o'clock in the morning. Arjun and Basanti wait for a bit on the outskirts of the village to make sure they have got all fifty goats together. Then they set off along a sandy track, driving the goats in front of them. The morning sun gets hotter as Arjun and Basanti are joined by other villagers with their moving herds. The track becomes a river of animals, ochre and cream-coloured cows, and black, white and brown goats. The track leads to barren wasteland with a few thorn bushes and, in the distance, rocky mountains. This area is known as the 'jungle' and when the animals reach it they all disperse in different directions. Arjun and Basanti usually have a rest on the ground when they have gone about half a mile—but it is never a long one as the goats go exploring all over the place looking for green leaves to eat.

All day long, with only short rests, Arjun and Basanti keep on the move, running after the goats with their sticks, making sure none gets lost.

Arjun seems to enjoy his life. 'I get bored sitting at home. I meet a lot of my friends out here in the "jungle". Sometimes we play kabaddi. One boy runs across to the other side to catch a boy and try and pull him across to his side without being caught. I'm good at it and catch quite a lot of boys. We also tell stories and jokes and things.

'I've had to deliver a baby goat out here. I learnt how to do it from a friend. I catch hold of the baby goat as it comes out and hold it round by its mother's face, and she licks it clean.'

Meanwhile, at home, Kani and the other women have tidied the place and washed up the breakfast things. Then they wrap up their chapattis and chillis for lunch and leave the toddlers with the grandparents. Then Kani straps her six month old daughter on to her back and goes off with the other women to join their husbands in the fields. If she is late she gets scolded by her husband and her mother-in-law.

Ghisa-Baba usually works at the well-head with his brother, driving the two pairs of oxen to irrigate the fields. As he does so he sings a yodelling chorus to the Water God to bring fertility to his land. Kani unties the baby from her back and puts her to sleep in a cradle made from material and slung on the end of the cart. Then she joins the other women as they cut the crop of green chick-peas and tie it into bundles, and then hoe the ground and weed it between the rows of wheat. Apart from a short lunch-break, the men and women work hard together all day.

The rabi crop is sown in November and is harvested in April. This
consists of wheat, barley, peas, radishes, carrots, mustard and chillis.
During the summer months it is too dry and hot for anything to grow.
But when the monsoon rains come in August the kharif crop is sown—
millet, maize, kidney-beans, black grain, sesame seeds. These are
harvested in November.

It takes two men and two pairs of bullocks to keep the land watered. One man stands at the well-head. He lowers the leather pouch into the well, lets it fill with water, and then winds it up by pulley. The other man guides the two pairs of bullocks up and down the ramp, sitting on the rope. This rope is tied at one end to the leather pouch and at the other end to the bullock's yoke. When the pouch gets to the top of the well-head, the water is tipped into irrigation channels which run through the fields. The oxen go round and round, up and down, and the water flows through the fields to the sound of singing. It is not just Ghisa-Baba who sings as he works at the well. All the farmers around Tilonia sing in the fields.

The sun begins to set at about 5 p.m., turning the sky red-gold as it sinks behind the mountains. This is the time when Arjun and Basanti gather their goats together and drive them back to the village. Then they put the goats in their pen and give them a meal of berries. Aunts, uncles, brothers, sisters and cousins all return from the fields at this time, with the cart, the two pairs of bullocks, the cows and the buffaloes. The animals are put in their pens and all the family help to feed them with green-stuff, clover and grass—and for each cow and bullock a bowl of meal. Later the animals are milked, water is fetched and family supper is cooked.

Arjun then has supper with his family, of wheat chapattis and liquid curd (like yogurt), as children do not drink chai, tea. And that is all he has after his energetic day out in the 'jungle'. Then he fetches his bag of books and is off to school, with the other boys who have to help their families in the fields. Arjun goes to the village middle school, following on from primary school, and this is free. The only time he gets to study is in the evening. There is also in Tilonia an all-age school where pupils aged six to sixteen study during the day-time.

By 7 p.m. Arjun and his companions are in their classrooms, sitting cross-legged in a circle on the floor with their slates balanced on their knees and their chalks ready to write. Each room is lit by several oil-lamps which cast a glow on the boys' faces peering from under their turbans.

At home and with his friends and family Arjun speaks a local language called Marwari. At this school they learn to read and write in Hindi, which is the main language spoken in India, especially in the north. They learn about the history and geography of India, and how it is governed today: about Rajasthan and Tilonia in particular, and about farming and how to look after animals. They also do maths and health education and hygiene, and learn which vegetables they should eat to keep well and stay strong.

When I asked Arjun one day about his school, he said, 'I enjoy it. I like maths best, especially multiplication tables—if you're good at maths the money-lenders can't cheat you! School helps me. It's good to be able to read and write too, because then nobody can make a fool of you.'

School for Arjun finishes at 9 p.m. He goes home and is in bed by 10 p.m. His day is long, and he always sleeps soundly after it.

In Tilonia the people are Hindus by religion. Ancient tradition divided Hindus into four main different castes, that is classes or kinds of people. The highest caste was that of the Brahmins. They were the priests—the religious leaders and teachers of the people. They knew the ancient Sanskrit language and recited all the books of the Vedas, sacred hymns written thirteen hundred years before the birth of Jesus.

To the next caste, the Kshatriyas, belonged many of the old Kings who were Rajputs. Some Rajputs are noblemen known as Thakurs. They used to own land and complete villages, and lived in great forts. Today their forts are falling in ruins and they no longer rule over people though they still own some land which they now have to farm themselves. The wives were kept in purdah (which means behind a veil) in separate women's rooms in their homes, and they were not allowed to go out except in a covered carriage.

Vaisyas, the third caste, were businessmen and merchants. Among them were Banias, money-lenders, and Sonars, silver-smiths, who make jewellery. In Rajasthan both women and men wear jewellery. A girl often wears ear-rings, a nose-ring, necklaces, bracelets, anklets and even toe-rings, all made of silver with precious stones. These represent her worldly wealth. The silver-smiths who make this jewellery and do repairs are fine craftsmen. Also, there are Kumhars, potters, who make and sell the large round earthenware pots for carrying water, earthenware cooking pots, and pottery oil-lamps which are burned during all religious festivals. Sometimes a potter is paid with grain instead of money. Nais, the barbers, are also Vaisyas in

this village. Nais are important people at ceremonies. The Nai carries the traditional letter, the 'patrika' from the bride to the groom at the wedding; he also carries out funeral rites and lights the funeral pyre on which by Hindu custom the body is burnt. 'Don't ever trust a Nai,' say the villagers, because he is supposed to be sly and cunning. Today many more kinds of people than before are traders and merchants, including the Malis and the Jats, to whom Arjun and his family belong. People say, 'An illiterate Jat thinks he is King, but a *literate* Jat is God himself!' In fact the Jats now have wealth and influence like that of the Rajputs of the olden days.

The fourth traditional caste, Sudras, included some groups of labourers and artisans. The Chamars, who were originally cobblers and shoe-makers, have given up that job because they believe leather is dirty, and now work as labourers on building sites, roads or farms. The Regars now work with leather and make and mend shoes. They also make the leather pouches for drawing water from wells. Regars treat the skins that are being turned into leather by being tanned, but they will not touch the dead animals from which the skins came.

The 'Untouchables' or Harijans (the Children of God as they were called by Gandhi) were outside and below the four castes. They do the work of collecting the dead oxen or buffaloes. They skin them, selling the skins to the Regars for tanning. By tradition Harijans get all the dirtiest jobs like sweeping streets and collecting rubbish. However, the Harijans in Tilonia are very resourceful and have started to breed pigs.

In the main street in Tilonia the Banias have a store where they sell cloth and grain, soap and cooking oil, and many other things. The Sonars have their shops in which silver and jewellery are displayed. Men, women, children and animals weave to and fro through the narrow streets. The busiest times are in the early morning and the evening, when the farmers and their families go to and from their work in the fields.

Most people in India are Hindus. Hindus believe in hundreds of different gods and goddesses, to whom they have built many temples and shrines. The most important of them are the gods Brahma, Vishnu, and Shiva, the goddesses Parvati and Lakshmi, and Ganesa the elephant god and Hanuman the monkey god.

Brahma is the Creator. Vishnu is the Protector. He changes himself into many forms that are also gods, like Krishna around whom there are legends of love and much poetry written and whose skin is dark blue. He is also Rama, brave and famous prince, the power of goodness who prevailed over evil when he slew the demon King Ravana in the epic legends, the Ramayana. Shiva is the God of the Dance (the Life-Force) but he is also the Destroyer. Lakshmi is Vishnu's wife, and she is the Goddess of Wealth. Parvati is married to Shiva. She is Shakti (that is Energy, the Life-Force) and she has a fierce form as Kali, the destroyer of evil, war and disease. As Durga, Parvati is usually shown as a beautiful lady riding a tiger or a lion.

Shiva and Parvati had a son called Karttikeya. Now Shiva was in the habit of going away for long periods to sit meditating on a mountain in the Himalayas. One legend relates how Parvati was having a bath during one of these absences and the perspiration in her hand grew into a little baby boy. She called him Ganesa. One day, when Ganesa was over a year old, Parvati asked him to guard the door while she took her bath, to make sure nobody disturbed her. It happened that on that day Shiva returned after his long absence. Ganesa did not know who he was, and when he saw him he said, 'You are not allowed in. My mother is having her bath.' Shiva was so furious at this that he cut off the boy's head with his sword. 'You don't know what you have done,' cried Parvati. 'You have killed my youngest son!' Stricken by grief, Shiva straightaway went out to look for another head for Ganesa. The first creature he met was an elephant. He chopped off its head, hurried back and placed the head on young Ganesa's body. Immediately the boy sprang to life again. So that is why Ganesa has an elephant's head on a human body.

One day Shiva wished to put his two children to the test to find out which of them would marry first. He invited them both to make a circle round the earth as quickly as they could. The eldest son Karttikeya mounted his peacock and made off at once with all speed. But Ganesa, taking his time about it, respectfully made a circle round his parents. When Shiva asked him why he did this, Ganesa replied, 'It is said in

the Rig Vedas that he who honours his parents by circling round them seven times has as much honour as he who circles the earth seven times.' And so he was the winner in the test.

Ganesa is one of the most popular Hindu gods. He is god of good luck, remover of obstacles. He is patron of learning and helps people to gain wealth and success. When Hindus do their Puja, worship, they must pray to Ganesa first before all the other gods. They light incense to him and bring offerings of flowers, coconuts, fruits and betel-nuts on leaves.

As well as the national gods and goddesses that people worship all over India, there are local gods and heroes. One of the most important of these in Rajasthan is Tejaji, a warrior hero to whom there are many shrines in Tilonia. Tejaji is said to have been born in Kharnar in Rajasthan. He was the son of a king, but both his parents died when he was a baby, and he was left in a field, wrapped in a cloth. A peasant woman found the baby and he was brought up by the farmer and his wife.

One day many years later when Tejaji was working in the fields, the farmer's wife came to him with his food, and said, 'If you want to eat bread prepared by the hand of a bride with red-painted hands, go to the house of your father-in-law and bring home your bride.'

So Tejaji went to the carpenter to get a cart made, bought a pair of bullocks, and set out with some of his friends to fetch his bride. On the way they saw two cobras being burnt in a fire. Tejaji took pity on them and managed to save one of the cobras from the flames. The cobra then insisted that it would have to bite Tejaji for not saving the other cobra too. So Tejaji promised to return to that place.

Then Tejaji went to the home of his father-in-law and was married to his beautiful daughter Sundar. But before he could take her to his home he said he had a duty to perform. On his way back to the place of the cobras he met an old lady in distress. 'Robbers have stolen my

bullocks,' she cried. 'Will you go and get them back for me?' So Tejaji
ran after the robbers and attacked them. Though he was wounded
with sword-cuts from head to foot he fought so bravely that he drove
the robbers off, recaptured the bullocks, and gave them back to the old
lady. Then, true to his word, he returned to the cobra. The cobra was
waiting to bite Tejaji, but when it saw his body covered with wounds, it
hesitated. Brave Tejaji held out his tongue. The cobra bit it. Tejaji was
poisoned by the bite and fell down and died.

It is said that Tejaji was given the power of restoring to life people
bitten by snakes. So people who have been bitten come to his shrines
today. They tie a thread round their right foot as they repeat the name
of Tejaji. Then they light incense and the priest sucks out the venom
from the bite. 'With the help of the power of Tejaji the person is always
cured,' I was assured.

In Susura, the town in which he died, there is a big statue and shrine
to Tejaji. There is a fair held there every year, when thousands of
people come to worship Tejaji and enjoy the Tejaji Mela. On the day of
the Mela a live cobra on a large bronze plate is placed in somebody's
house. Pilgrims come with little earthenware dishes of milk which they
offer to the cobra. They light incense and ask for the cobra's blessing.
They believe that Tejaji has come to help them in the form of this live
snake.

As there are many Indian gods and goddesses, there are many religious festivals every year. There are national festivals like Divali and Holi, and local festivals for the local gods and heroes. One of these is the festival of Ghasbabba, God of Protection of Tilonia, which takes place once a year.

On the evening of the day of this festival, the people of Tilonia dress up in their best clothes. The men and boys put on new brightly-coloured turbans of crimson red, purple or saffron yellow, with fresh white dhotis and shirts. The women and girls dress in brilliant shawls, veils, blouses and skirts of red, yellow and purple, patterned with gold thread, embroidery and sequins. They decorate their hair and wear all their finest jewellery—earrings, necklaces, nose-rings, bracelets, anklets and toe-rings, so that they glitter like queens. At about 9.30 p.m. when it is dark, people leave their homes and walk in procession to the edge of the village. The men and boys go in front, with the women and girls

behind, singing together. Male and female drummers, specially hired for the occasion, beat out their rhythms. The people gather round a black stone, which is mounted on two blocks of wood, and has been painted white for the occasion. Torchbearers come with flaming torches, and some people carry lamps to light up the scene.

The Brahmin priest stands by the stone. The drum-beats and the women's singing dies down. The priest says some mantras, or prayers, and then holds out a mirror in front of two eyes painted on the stone. At this point the mirror shatters into pieces and it is said that the spirit of Ghasbabba the God of Protection enters into the stone. Everyone drums and sings, and the first of several pairs of oxen that are ready is harnessed to the stone. It is a great honour for a farmer who has oxen big and strong enough to pull it.

The stone is heaved on to a wooden base and dragged round the village. The oxen are changed regularly because of the weight of the stone and because other farmers want the honour of pulling it. At the head of the procession are the oxen driven by the farmer, then the priest walking behind, followed by crowds of happy people singing and drumming. In this way Ghasbabba the God, who has entered the stone, blesses and protects the men, women, children, animals and homes of Tilonia for another year.

Arjun thoroughly enjoys festivals like this one. But it only happens once a year. 'I like music and songs,' he said to me one day, 'and I like going to Bhajans.' A Bhajan is a gathering of the villagers, mostly men, older women and children, at which there are music and drums and singing. It is not a festival but a get-together to sing praises to the gods. Bhajans go on all night. Arjun explained that the songs are usually by Mira, who sang songs in praise of Lord Krishna. The villagers also sing to Rama.

I asked Arjun if he wanted to get married. 'Nai,' he said, 'I don't want to. When I grow up I want to be a farmer, and specially to work at the well. And I want to have four bullocks of my own.'